Mother's REJECTION

BLACK SPERM MAKES BLACK BABIES

ESTER SUTTON SULLIVAN

Copyright © 2023 Ester Sutton Sullivan.

All rights reserved. No part of this book may be reproduced, stored, or transmitted by any means—whether auditory, graphic, mechanical, or electronic—without written permission of both publisher and author, except in the case of brief excerpts used in critical articles and reviews. Unauthorized reproduction of any part of this work is illegal and is punishable by law.

ISBN: 979-8-89031-363-8 (sc)
ISBN: 979-8-89031-364-5 (hc)
ISBN: 979-8-89031-365-2 (e)

Because of the dynamic nature of the Internet, any web addresses or links contained in this book may have changed since publication and may no longer be valid. The views expressed in this work are solely those of the author and do not necessarily reflect the views of the publisher, and the publisher hereby disclaims any responsibility for them.

One Galleria Blvd., Suite 1900, Metairie, LA 70001
1-888-421-2397

MOTHERS

TO

BE

MOTHERS   *MOTHERS*

MOTHERS

*MOTHER, BE SURE
OF YOUR CHOICE.*

*MOTHER, IT IS
YOUR DECISION.*

*MOTHER, CHECK
WITHIN YOUR HEART
BEFORE DATING.*

If there are not going to be any children, may God bless you in your relationship.

I turned out okay in this black skin because I had no color. I was taught that I could be and do anything in life that I chose, and that I was beautiful. I am black, Irish white, and Choctaw Indian. I was baptized as a Christian at the age of nine. God has been my father and has been here for me all my life. When I grew weak at different stages in life, he (God) carried me. I am blessed and thankful.

NO ONE SHOULD EVER HAVE A STORY LIKE THIS TO WRITE ABOUT. I WRITE BECAUSE I HOPE THIS WRITING WILL SAVE A FEW CHILDREN FROM HAVING TO EXPERIENCE THIS TYPE OF LIFE. I WOULD NOT WISH IT ON ANYONE, FOR THEY MAY NOT BE AS LUCKY OR BLESSED AS I WAS AND AS I AM. BUT I WILL NEVER HAVE THE KNOWLEDGE OF A MOTHER'S LOVE. NO BABY NEEDS THIS EXPERIENCE.

Black sperm makes black babies. If you know that all of your life you did not like black children and black females, then do not punish a newborn baby; just don't.

When I asked my mother why she did not want me because she was married to my father, my ears and heart were waiting for her answer, and I quote her answer: **"You were so black, just so black. When my first baby was born, he** *looked like a peach. I knew that I did not want another black baby and if I kept putting something black into me something black might come out, and that is why I left your dad. He told me that if I was going to leave, I could not take his children. So I left you and your brother. It hurt me to leave you all, but I could not take the chance of being with a black man again, so I left."*

I was eighteen months old, and my brother was three years old. My dad came home from work to find us alone. I was told he worked at the air force base. He left us with his mother during

MOTHER'S REJECTION

the day and picked us up for the night to be with him. Daddy got in touch with our mother's mother. She sold her home and land where she lived. She brought her animals and chickens with her.

I remember the cow and the bell around her neck.

This grandmother purchased a plot of land with a long, white shotgun house on it.

I do not know how long it took her to get all this completed, but between the two grandmothers, they kept us with daddy, transporting us back and forth. All I remember is the love from both of them.

By the time we started school, we were living with my mother's mother. She was a big woman, a Choctaw Indian woman with hair down her shoulders. She was a brown Indian woman with a pretty face, and she worked hard to keep my brother and me clean and fed. We were happy and wanted to do anything that we could to help.

My grandmother had a garden, a chicken for eggs, and a cow for milk.

I remember she brought pigs and we fed and watered them, and when they were large enough they were killed for meat. My grandmother had a smokehouse where she hung meat from the beams in the ceiling.

My brother and I were happy, and we loved our grandma dearly.

Then one day, here came this woman and a baby. My grandmother told us that this lady was our mother. I remember holding on to my grandmother, because we did not know this lady. Five years had passed, and she had never come around, and our grandmother was our mother.

This woman was a light-skinned woman with long hair, and this little girl was light-skinned with long hair. My mother did not live with us; she lived on my daddy's land in his house. She asked her mother to keep this child during the day while she worked. She would get off the bus in front of our house and pick up her little girl. And this was a good arrangement because they did not live with us. But little did I know my grandmother loved her daughter, and she let her bring that little girl to live in our house when she became school age.

It would have been okay, except she was so bad. She would not obey our grandmother, and she would curse her and my brother. I wanted to hurt her, but we knew better; this would hurt our kindhearted grandmother. So we learned to dislike her. If she had not loved her daughter, she would not have cared for my brother and me.

Every other weekend, our daddy picked my brother and me up and carried us to spend the weekend with his mother, which we enjoyed. Before this, grandma came. We spent every day with his mother while he worked. When I was nine years old, my father's mother was hit by a car, which was a hit-and-run. Later another car came along and ran over something, and it was my grandmother. She never regained conscious, and she died.

This was so sad. My brother and I really missed her. We missed her for a long time.

Being young, you do not forget, but time heals the wound and you move on with the living to be done.

My mother moved into the house with us. She was pregnant and about to deliver in a few weeks. I remember going to get the midwife; it was a boy. This was not so bad. She left the baby with my grandmother and went back to her house, which was good. But about two years later, here she came again. She was pregnant and ready to deliver. I went and got the same midwife; it was another boy.

By this time my grandma had had a stroke and could not take care of this

MOTHER'S REJECTION

child. My mother gave him away the same day that he was born. My grandma had me take a clean white cloth and put sugar in it, tie a knot, and dip it in warm water, making a sugar tip for the baby to suck on until the ladies got off work and came to pick him up. My mother already had this planned; she knew that she did not want to keep a baby.

I was glad because the other little boy was about two and a half years old.

My mother had beaten my oldest brother until he was bleeding. He had fallen asleep in the movies. When the janitor was cleaning he woke my brother up.

My mother met him coming home and beat him all the way. He was bleeding badly. My grandma got her shotgun and pointed it at her daughter and said to her, "If you hit him again, I will kill you," so she quit. My brother was about eleven years old, and my mother was saying, "You are not going to be like your daddy." It was sad around the home for a few weeks until my mother left and went back to her house.

My grandma asked her sister to keep my brother because my mother seemed to hate him too. When my aunt came to get my brother, there was so much sadness. But this kept my grandmother from killing

MOTHER'S REJECTION

her daughter. You see, this was this black man's child, even if he was her husband.

My grandma married a white Irish man who was killed when my grandma was seven months pregnant with my mother, and my grandmother spoiled my mother all her life, even up to just months before her death. My mother would come by and con her out of money. My grandma was seventy-three years old when she died, and my mother never did let up.

A newborn baby needs and deserves the love of a mother. Thank God for grandmothers; they die, get sick, and have strokes, and their blood pressure rises.

This is okay, because they have raised their children and should not have to be burdened with grandchildren unless the parents die or there is an unusual stressful need. Grandchildren are to be a blessing coming and going.

A newborn should never be rejected by its parents, especially the mother who carried it nine months. But when this happens, that is why there are adoptions. Adoptions can be a beautiful thing because the child is wanted, loved, and chosen.

When the mother is in a relationship with the father—mostly this black father—and the relationship is over, the mother no longer wants the child or the children. Some mothers may keep the children to draw a check—still no love. The child or children can feel this. This is where they become prey for adults and relatives who are aware of the situation. The mother is not in tune and simple does not care. The living grandmother is no longer any use to her, because she can no longer take care of her children.

After the stroke, grandma needed someone to take care of her.

I had high self-esteem because my grandmother (the dark-skinned, long-haired Choctaw Indian), who was my mother's mother, always made me feel beautiful about myself; she was awesome. She instilled in me the notion that I could do anything and everything that I put my mind to.

I remember coming home from school after starting the first grade and pulling off my school clothes and hanging them up so they would not get wrinkles and could be worn again.

I always had to wash my hands after changing, so I would not bring in germs from school. We still had to look nice in case of company coming to see my grandma.

We would go outside and do chores alone with grandma. This was fun no matter what had to be done, because she was teaching us to do many things. After eating dinner, I would help her clean up the kitchen. Then grandma would call out to get our schoolwork, and if I did not have any, she would say, "Bring a book and read to me." I loved reading to her, for in a little while I would have to wake her up; she was tried from all the work by this time of night.

But we still had to brush our teeth and run the bath water so that we would be clean for the next day. This was a practice for the next five years, until she had the stroke. That is when life changed for me; I was eleven years old at that time and going into the sixth grade.

The unique experience and personal relationships that I had with both my grandmothers built high self-esteem and has lasted throughout my life. I liked my teachers and classmates at my first school.

I made good grades. My high self-esteem helped me to have more to offer during this change of life, which was unfamiliar to me with new ideas and ways of doing things. The only comfort I had was that my grandmother was there, which was probably the biggest reason for my being there. I was to be her little nurse and caregiver. I had to feed and clean her before going to school in the mornings, and I was late most of the time, which I hated.

I had to walk to a new school in the city. If I was late in the morning, the rule was that I had to make up the time that evening. I got in trouble at home for being late coming home. If my aunt missed her bus for work, it made her late, and I got a whipping for being late. I let this go on for three years; I was so tried of the whippings.

There were two children in the home—a four-year-old and a three-month-old, my little cousins. I had to babysit them at night and change the baby's diaper and give it a bottle in the morning, along with the duties for my grandmother, before going to school. I loved her so much I did not mind doing this for her.

The way I was able to be included in this family with my grandmother this was her youngest daughter.

My mother tried to put my grandmother in a nursing home, and one of the ladies working at the nursing home was a friend of my mother's sister, and she called her and told what my mother was trying to do with her mother. My grandmother had four daughters. The other three got very angry at my mother. The youngest daughter was in her thirties. She came that evening and took her mother to her home to keep her.

I cried and wanted to go with my grandma, but my aunt said no because my mother could cause trouble for my aunt if she took her child. I was left behind for my mother to deal with.

My mother had her plans. A few weeks later my mother got a lady to keep her daughter while she was away.

My mother took her little son with her. She was going to my grandmother's sister's home to visit her son. This was my brother, whom she had beaten years earlier.

We went to the city bus station, which was the Greyhound bus station. She brought their tickets and sat down and waited for the bus to arrive in her town. My mother gave me a one-dollar bill. When the bus arrived, she and my little brother, who was four years old, got on the bus. My mother waved goodbye to me and said, "Be a good girl," and the bus drove off.

My heart began to hurt; I had never been to this large bus station before. People were all over the place, and they would have never guessed that this little black girl had been with that whitish looking lady and the light-skinned boy who had just left.

When my grandma used to pray, I would kneel down beside her and listen to her pray. I joined church when I was nine years old. Oh yes, I did believe in Jesus.

A few tears came streaming down my cheeks, but I could not go on crying; I thought, "What am I going to do before people notice that I am alone?"

I remembered my aunt's phone number—Regency 60849—so I dialed it, and my aunt next to my mother answered the phone.

I told her where I was and what had happened, and she asked me if I had any money. I said, "Yes, one dollar." She told me to catch a cab and come to 608 N. Geary St.

This was where my grandma lived. You could ride a cab for twenty-five cents for miles. This aunt lived upstairs in the same building.

My aunt who was keeping my grandma was at work. My grandma and my aunt gave me hugs and kisses when I arrived.

But I was wondering what my other aunt would say. I guess they all talked and saw how I could help out by being there. So this was where I stayed.

When my mother returned from her trip and came by to get money from my grandma, I opened the door and she said, "You little bitch, I thought I had got rid of you." *I guess she thought I was black without a brain. My mother's other sisters had lighter skin and longer hair than she.*

My grandmother married an Indian and Frenchman for her second husband, and they had three girls. They all married dark-skinned black men in the military—army and navy. No one had this problem with color but my mother. Her father was Irish white and had been killed for marring my grandmother.

By the time my mother decided that she could not stand little black babies, the damage was done. I was born and was to depend on a mother for everything. In my case her decision affected not only my life, but my brother's life as well, because he is eighteen months older than I and we have the same father, which is my mother's husband. This is why it is so important that all human beings search their soul as to what skin color really means to them, especially when considering a relationship with a black man or woman.

If you think you want a relationship with a black, ask yourself how you feel about being black yourself. You need the answer to this question, because if there are children, you will need to be able to love and care for these children for the rest of your life; they will forever be a part of you.

Think about whether your parents want to be grandparents to your mixed-race child or children. Will their cousins want to play with them or even own them as their relatives? Remember back to what your own sisters and brothers said about blacks, Negros, or Niger when you were growing up.

In your own heart, be true to yourself. Honesty is the only way, because it may come back to interfere in your child's life later.

Yes, it is the skin, because all babies are born beautiful on the inside. It is what is in the eyes and heart of the beholder, especially the parents of the child. Most often, it is particularly the mother. When the mother loves, care for, and fulfills the needs of her child at birth, the gap will be closed for the child ever having to know the feeling of being in need. When a mother loves her own children, the family or people who love her will also love the children, for they are a part of her.

The father's role is very important also, but in a different way. He is the source of where they came from, the provider, someone who goes and comes each day.

The father's presence makes such a difference in his little girl's eyes; he is a giant. Even when she surely loves her mother, it takes years for her to reveal the feeling that she has for her mother. Most girls need their daddy's love. This help keeps them from being so needy for boys' affection when they become teenagers.

They know the love of their father's arms. This seems to make such a difference in young women's decision making throughout their lives when it comes to the man in their lives—whom to choose and whom not to choose. The girls also want the approval of their father about the choices they make.

Yes, the baby boy or son needs a father for an altogether different reason, but one just as important, or even more important. He needs the love of his model, someone to be an example while he is growing up. The son is very close to his mother, but for a different reason than that of his dad. It is so important for the mother and father to be present in their children's lives from birth to the completion of at least college.

(This is in a same-nationality marriage.) Can you argue the need for parents in a mixed marriage, with one of the parents being black or African American, the need for this marriage to be for better or worse, until death do them part? It is a must. The children suffer when a mixed marriage with one of the parents being black or African American splits.

The mother's own race does not want the responsibility of helping with the children.

There is a constant fear of a new friend or parent requiring or demanding a sadistic move on your child or children. When the black parent leaves the home, most of the time the remaining parent does not want the mixed children or black-skinned kids. Oh yes! They may be worth drawing a check. Let me check Social Services; that may be worth my while. They can be good for something.

I have seen the little children being pushed around in the grocery store, half dressed, noses running.

My heart goes out to them because it is not their fault. I think about how lucky I was to have a loving grandmother to come and see about me when my mother left me because, as she said, I was so black. I was in my fifties when she made the statement. She could not take the chance of having another black child.

I have to keep thanking my grandmothers for their love. God replaced the mother with the kind of love that caused me to develop physically and mentally, with emotions. My father's mother shared her love on weekends, and her home was like a vacation, and there I learned in a different way, without chores. She would take us to church with her and let us help her fix food and set the table—that is all we could do; she lived in the city. Then we learned about death and the emotional period of sadness that comes from losing a love one.

We had to accept change, for that part of life was over. But we had established lifelong memories of this grandmother's love.

During this stage of life, my brother and I needed my other grandma to help us move on mentally. I remember that she shared with us something that helped her when her mother passed away. We got the chance to ask questions about death.

We began to do even better in school, and the hurt soon went away.

I am seventy now, and I still remember the beautiful memories of both of my loving and giving grandmothers. I thank God for his helpers being right on time in the form of grandmothers. I could write on about this hand that I was dealt. But I have moved on, and life is good.

My point in this writing is for other young females and males to think twice before having sex with a black man or woman. Think about what will happen to the children if there is a separation or divorce.

When both parents are together as a family, the children's skin color does not matter; it is after or between the parents so there is no rejection.

The black race is the only race that makes this big difference, and the children suffer.

This black skin of mind covers a three-part person with a personality of each of these cultures. Since I like myself so much and I am so thankful for me, I believe that I must have been dealt the best of each culture. It is kind of like a chocolate-covered piece of candy; choose your own kind as long as it is covered with chocolate. I had to have God's favor to be this loner that I was. No matter how many people were around, I was still a loner, never really connecting with anyone completely. I am sure this came from not trusting as a young child.

This was and is okay because I've always had Jesus to talk to and keep me company. I know he is the only one who really knows me. After my grandma had her stroke and I had to help care for her, that left me no one here on earth to trust. I was eleven years old, and everyone called on me to do this and do that. I remember crying sometimes, but then I would call out, "I am coming!"

Here is what kept me going: I was a loner, but I was never lonely; I always had Jesus as my father, and we talked about everything. He is the best friend you can have.

In today's world, mixed couples are marrying more than ever before. I find nothing wrong with this if the mother loves her baby no matter what, with or without the father. The problem is when the mother has a problem with her own child.

Among my own children, there is mixed marriage. The couple has become one, and this is what marriage is about. I thank God for my first set; all of their children have graduated from college. I pray the next set will do the same.

My first grandchild to marry is part of a mixed couple. My daughter tells me that she could not have wished for a son-in-law to love her daughter more. This is a blessing, and I know that my granddaughter will love her children unconditionally.

If there are not going to be any children, may God bless you in your relationship.

In case you get pregnant by a black man, give the baby life. If you are sure that you do not want the baby because of color or whatever other reason, please give it up for adoption so it can have a chance to be loved. If you do not want to go through the paperwork just leave the baby in the hospital. Put a note in the baby's crib saying "PLEASE FIND THIS BABY A GOOD HOME. THANK YOU."

You will not be in trouble with the law if you do it this way. You will make a mother very happy.

Most of all, the important thing is that you will be able to live with yourself.

May God bless you, and good luck.

TO MY SIX CHILDREN

WITH LOVE

FIVE SONS AND ONE SPECIAL DAUGHTER

Each one of you was special at birth and had your own space.

Even until graduation of the twelfth grade

I had a curfew hour to be home.

I wanted each of you to be the best at whatever your choice.

Mothers, enjoy your babies, because they grow up quickly.

ABOUT THE AUTHOR

She is a mother of six children; three sons, one daughter, two sons. An ex-wife of a retired Flight Engineer Instructor. She has a degree in Psychology and a minor in Sociology; Forty Seven units in Teaching Credentials. She is working in a Computer Lab. She is a survivor of breast cancer for fourteen years, the praise be to God. She is the Author of CANCER IS JUST RIGHT FOR GOD. This book will help you understand that by the grace of God you can be and do anything you put your mind too. She has so much hope for living and writing to be done. May this reading give you hope in what ever you want to do, just get started. Thanks for reading.

www.ingramcontent.com/pod-product-compliance
Lightning Source LLC
LaVergne TN
LVHW092100060526
838201LV00047B/1486